AIDEN and AALIYAH

Sharing Is Caring

Julia Harrison

PAGE PUBLISHING, INC.
Conneaut Lake, PA

First originally published by Page Publishing 2021

ISBN 978-1-6624-2938-5 (pbk)
ISBN 978-1-6624-2939-2 (digital)

Printed in the United States of America

To my sweet children Caison, Zamorah and Zhiya. Thank you for helping me find my passion and purpose. I love you.

It was a beautiful sunny afternoon. Aiden and Aaliyah were playing tag out back when Mom shouted, "Who wants cookies?"

Aiden and Aaliyah were so excited to eat their cookies. They ran inside of the house to wash their hands.

After sitting down at the table, they both shouted hooray when they saw the delicious cookies. "Oh no!" Aaliyah cried.

4

Aaliyah accidentally knocked all of her cookies to the ground. Aiden looked over to his sister and had an idea.

5

"Don't cry, have some of my cookies." Aaliyah was happy again as they both shared Aiden's cookies.

Later that day, Aiden was playing with his building blocks while Aaliyah colored a picture. Aiden was trying to build a tower, but it kept tumbling down.

He became frustrated and very sad that he couldn't build his tower. Aaliyah looked over at her brother and had an idea.

8

"Aiden, can I help you build your tower?" she asked. Once they worked together to build the tower, it did not fall, and Aiden was very happy.

The sun went down, and the stars lit the night sky. It was almost time to go to sleep. Mom reminded Aaliyah and Aiden to feed their goldfish before bedtime.

They both raced to the fishbowl, and Aaliyah grabbed the fish food. "I'm going to feed the fish," Aaliyah said. "No, I want to feed the fish!" Aiden shouted.

The two began arguing over the food. Mom heard Aiden and Aaliyah arguing, so she walked over and saw what was going on. Then Mom had an idea.

"Why don't you both feed the fish together?" Mom suggested. They all smiled as Mom helped them take some food out and sprinkle it into the fishbowl.

After prayer, Mom tucked them both to bed and kissed them good night. Before she left, she told them both, "Even if it may be hard sometimes, it's nice to share with others because it makes everyone happy."

Aiden and Aaliyah smiled. "Good night, Mom," they both said. "Sweet dreams. I love you both," Mom replied.

The End

About the Author

Julia Harrison, a mother of three, is a young entrepreneur and newly published children's book author. Motherhood inspired her to begin writing a series of African American children's books that promote positive narratives, teaches a variety of morals and values while encouraging self-reflection. The Aiden and Aaliyah children's book series is the modern-day antidote to Julia's childhood and the lack of exposure to positive influences that she could physically relate to in books and media. Growing up as a Brooklyn native, Julia's lived experiences motivated her to write about her daily musings and to begin expressing her feelings on paper, which led to a love of journalism.

CPSIA information can be obtained
at www.ICGtesting.com
Printed in the USA
JSHW051305091221
21049JS00010B/39